Elaine Knox-Wagner

THE OLDEST KID

Pictures by Gail Owens

ALBERT WHITMAN & COMPANY, CHICAGO

Library of Congress Cataloging in Publication Data

Knox-Wagner, Elaine.
  The oldest kid.

  (Concept books/level 1)
  SUMMARY: Burdened by her position as oldest child in
the family, a little girl finally learns there are
privileges, too.
  [1. Brothers and sisters—Fiction] I. Owens, Gail.
II. Title
PZ7.K77801   [E]   81-294
ISBN 0-8075-5986-5   AACR1

*To first kids who sometimes feel last
and to a third kid named Alan who's my friend*

Ever since I was born,
I've been the oldest kid.

It's not fair.

Being oldest means
I got to our house first.
It means my room and toys
and dad and mom
were all mine—

until my brother came.

Then I had to share.
EVERYTHING.
Even the big map on my bedroom wall.
(He ate half of Africa.)

Being oldest means I have to set a good example.
When I want another ride on the merry-go-round
and my folks say, "No, just one today,"
I climb off my favorite horse right away.

My brother screams
and hangs onto his horse's neck so hard
my dad has to PEEL him off.

If I did that, I'd probably get traded in
like our old car.

Being oldest means I should
mind the teacher and get A's
and be an engineer like my dad
and make my bed without wrinkles
and say "Thank you" and "Please"
and never hit little kids
or do ANYthing wrong.

It's not fair.

In the summer, we have picnics
at Grandma and Grandpa Wentworth's.
The kids eat first.
Only ten fit at the picnic table.

Guess who's the oldest cousin?
Guess who makes eleven?
Guess who waits to eat?

At Sunday's picnic, I got mad.
There I am, starving.

"I want a place on the bench,"
I tell my grandma.

"You can eat with the grown-ups,"
she says.

"But I want to eat now," I say.
"I can't wait."

"Don't be silly," says my dad,
spooning dribble off my brother's chin.
"Go talk to your grandpa for a bit."

I grab a pickle so I won't starve to death.

Grandpa is working on his car.
It's very old and shiny black.
Grandma says it has first place in his heart.
She means he really likes it.

"I hate being the oldest kid,"
I tell him. "It's not fair."

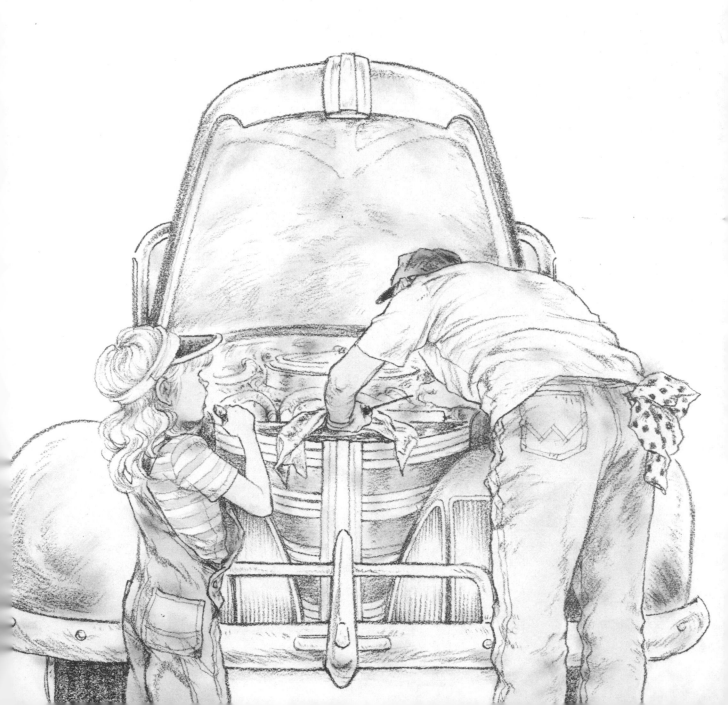

He nods and hands me a screwdriver.

"I can't even eat with the other kids," I say.
"There's no room for me."

He nods again and hands me a wrench.

"I'm a kid, too," I say.
"Mmmm," he says. "Would you aim
this flashlight right over there?"

I put the screwdriver in my hat.
Then I aim the light so he can see.

"Just as I thought," he says. "Wrench?"
I hand him the wrench.
"Screwdriver?"

He takes it from my hat.

He clamps the wrench around a bolt.
He tries to use the screwdriver
with his other hand.

"By jiminy," he says.
"Can't do both at once."

"I can help," I say.

He nods. "Okay.
You hold this wrench.
Don't let it slip."

Grandpa turns the screwdriver.
I use both hands and all my muscles
to hold the wrench still.

Just when I think
I can't hold it any longer,
Grandpa says, "That's it, Pal.
We dood it."

We close the hood carefully,
put our tools back where they belong,
and wipe our hands on rags.

"Hey, Marge," Grandpa calls to my grandma.
"We're going out for a spin.
Got to roadtest this repair job."

All the cousins who can walk and talk
jump up from the table.
They run toward us.
"Me, too! Me, too!" they yell.

"Not this time, kids," Grandpa says.
"Not this time."

He backs the car slowly down the
driveway. The cousins run after us.

"You think you're so smart,"
my nasty cousin yells at me.
"Just because you're oldest,
you get to do EVERYthing."

"Finish eating," says Grandpa.
"You'll have your turn later."

As we drive, Grandpa listens
to the engine.
I keep quiet so he can hear.
We drive around the lake
and through downtown
and out to the highway.

"Runs like a top," he says finally.
"We did a good job on it, Pal."
He lets me turn on the radio
as we head back to the house.

Ever since I was born,
I've been the oldest kid.
It's hardly ever fair.
But sometimes it feels fair.

ELAINE KNOX-WAGNER is an oldest kid. Sometimes it feels fair. She lives in the Highland Park area of St. Paul, Minnesota. Formerly the director of a small manufacturing company in Los Angeles, Elaine chose writing as her second career, a career she loves. As a reporter, she has won nine writing awards, six of them for educational articles. She also writes essays, poetry, short stories, and magazine articles and has won various awards in these areas. She likes kids—oldest, youngest, middle, or in-between—and is the mother of Mike, Kelly, and Gwen, who are grown-up now and gone from home. Elaine is skinny, has grey hair and green eyes and spaces between her front teeth. She talks a lot, is curious, and likes hamburgers and onion rings. Everyone in the world doesn't love her. Which is hardly fair, she says.

GAIL OWENS was born and reared in Detroit, Michigan. She lived in New York City for about thirteen years, then moved to the Mid-Hudson Valley area. She has two children. Gail has always worked in the commercial art field—as designer, art director, and illustrator. She has illustrated over forty books for children.